Book design by Andrea Fronc
Illustrated by Bob Berry, Tom Brannon, Warner McGee, and Sesame Workshop
Edited by Susan Rich Brooke

Published by Phoenix International Publications, Inc.
8501 West Higgins Road, Suite 300, Chicago, Illinois 60631
Lower Ground Floor, 59 Gloucester Place, London WIU 8JJ

www.pikidsmedia.com

p i kids is a trademark of Phoenix International Publications, Inc.,
and is registered in the United States.

Look and Find is a trademark of Phoenix International Publications, Inc., and
is registered in the United States and Canada.

8 7 6 5 4 3 2 1

ISBN: 978-1-5037-2611-6

Table of Contents

Dance with Elmo! ▶ ▶ ▶ ▶ ▶ ▶ ▶ ▶ ▶ ▶ ▶ ▶ ▶

To see Elmo dance, hold the bottom-right corner of the book's inside pages firmly in your hand, with your thumb on the top of the first page and your fingers on the bottom of the last page.

Now, press down with your thumb so the corner bends. Then drag your thumb down the corner of the pages so that the pages flip up. The faster you move your thumb, the faster Elmo will dance.

To see Elmo dance in reverse, put your fingers on the top of the first page and your thumb on the bottom of the last page. Then drag your thumb up the corner of the pages so that the pages flip down.

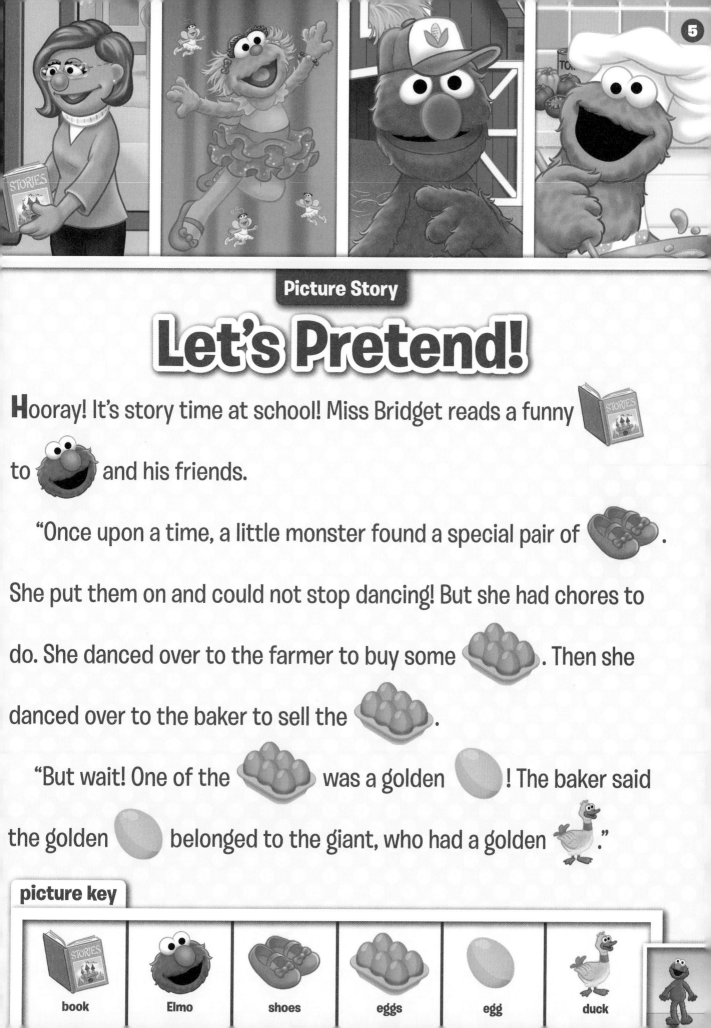

Picture Story

Let's Pretend!

Hooray! It's story time at school! Miss Bridget reads a funny [book] to [Elmo] and his friends.

"Once upon a time, a little monster found a special pair of [shoes]. She put them on and could not stop dancing! But she had chores to do. She danced over to the farmer to buy some [eggs]. Then she danced over to the baker to sell the [eggs].

"But wait! One of the [eggs] was a golden [egg]! The baker said the golden [egg] belonged to the giant, who had a golden [duck]."

picture key

book	Elmo	shoes	eggs	egg	duck

"Then what happens?" asks . So Miss Bridget turns

the page of the 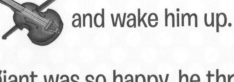 and reads some more.

"The dancing monster danced up, up,

up a beanstalk to give the golden

to the giant. The giant was fast asleep, so

the dancing monster asked a musician to

play the and wake him up.

"The giant was so happy, he threw a party. The baker brought

lots of . After the party, the little monster was too tired

to dance home. So the giant called

a , and the monster got

home safe and sound! Everybody

lived happily ever after."

As the story ends, the 🔔 rings for recess!

At recess, (Zoe) pretends to be a dancer with special 👟.

(Grover) pretends to be a farmer gathering 🥚.

(Cookie Monster) pretends to be a baker who bakes 🍕.

(Big Bird) pretends to be a musician who plays 🎻.

(Abby) pretends to drive a 🚕.

"What are you pretending to be, ?" asks (Abby).

(Elmo) climbs up, up, up to the top of the slide and calls down,

"Fee-fi-fo-fum, 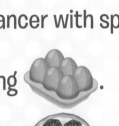 is a GIANT. Here he comes!"

---

picture key

🔔 bell	Zoe	👟 shoes	Grover	🥚 eggs	Cookie Monster
🍕 pizza	Big Bird	🎻 violin	Abby	🚕 taxi	Elmo

Rapunzel's World

Princess Rapunzel lives way up high in a tower. She was locked up by a witch who wants to keep her away from the world.

Rapunzel's life could be boring. There isn't anywhere to go or anything much to do in the tower. But Rapunzel discovers that she can go anywhere and do anything…in her imagination. And so she does! She looks out her window and imagines living in the kingdom that she can see down below.

Rapunzel imagines herself going to school, playing with friends in the park, having fun at a party, and shopping at the grocery store. (Even princesses have to eat.) It's fun to imagine!

One day, a brave prince arrives to help Rapunzel escape. He climbs up the tower wall, and then he and Rapunzel climb down together. "Everything out here is going to be strange and new to you," the prince says. "Aren't you a little…scared?" Rapunzel laughs. "I can't imagine being scared," she says, "but I can imagine being happy. And now I really will be. Kingdom, here I come!"

Adventurous Boaters

brought to you by the letters **A** and **B**. Tap each one you find!

BIRD

ART

BEAR

BERT

BUG

BALL

BED

ARM

APPLE

BOX

All any adventure needs is a best buddy, a box, and a big imagination!

What Else Could It Be?

Elmo sees a paper bag.
What could it become?
A puppet with big googly eyes
and one long wiggly tongue!

Ernie sees a newspaper.
What else could it be?
A hat to wear when Ernie goes
a-sailing on the sea!

Grover sees some cardboard tubes.
What could they become?
A trumpet in a marching band
and sticks to play a drum!

Abby sees a shoebox.
What else could it be?
A house where dollie Annie lives,
where friends can share some tea.

WHAT'S DIFFERENT?

If you can't get to the beach to swim, hop under the fire hose and pretend! Look for 5 differences between these splashy scenes.

Welcome to the Potty Award Show!
Can you find these potty prizes?

Abby's Potty Show

Diddle-diddle-dotty!
    Abby's on the potty.
If going potty takes some time,
    Abby says this little rhyme:

"I can read. I can sing.
    I can wiggle fairy wings!
And if I haven't gone quite yet,
    I can say the alphabet!"

Abby's rhyme helps her to wait.
    Then she's done—and she did great!
Abby imagines that when you go,
    you star in your own potty show!

1st Position

B is for Ballerina

Grand Jeté

Dancing with the Twiddlebugs

Dance class is about to begin! Zoe is pretending to be Mademoiselle Zoe, the prima ballerina. She is teaching the Twiddlebugs how to dance for a performance of "Snow White and the Seven Twiddlebugs."

"The first step is a pirouette," says Zoe. "Get up on your tippy toes and spin. And a-one, and a-two..."

As soon as the Twiddlebugs start to spin, their little wings flap and they float up, up, up into the air.

"Uh-oh," says Zoe. "Let's glissade instead. Step, then glide! Step, then glide!"

When the Twiddlebugs glide, they start to fly again!

"How can I teach you to dance if you can't keep your feet down on the ground?" asks Zoe.

Zoe tries something new. "Let's do a grand jeté," she says to the Twiddlebugs. "I'll demonstrate." She leaps up into the air. "Oh, this feels like flying!" Zoe says. "Let's all fly together!"

Now it's time for the performance! The orchestra begins to play. The curtain rises. The Twiddlebug dancers flit and fly around the stage. Zoe leaps up high, soars across the stage, and lands right beside...Elmo?

"Hi, Elmo," Zoe giggles. "What are you doing here? I didn't know you were a famous dancer!"

"You can be whoever you want to be when you pretend," says Elmo, as the audience claps wildly.

"Ah, yes, greetings! It is I, the Count, in the Wild Wild West with Elmo and Grover. I can't stop counting, even when I'm pretending to be a cowboy! Can you count in the scene along with me?"

1 cowboy hat

2 sheriff's stars

3 cactus plants

4 cowboy boots

5 lovely lizards

All Day Long

Picture Story

Wake Up, !

The  is up, but  isn't, until...**STRUMMM! COOOO!**

"What's making all that noise?"  wonders. He hops out of

bed to find out.

Outside, a cheery  is shining down on  and .

"It's a great day," says . "I just had to play a song to let

everybody know!"

While  **STRUMS** his , a  starts to **COO**.

"Wow!" says . "The  is singing along."

picture key

Elmo	sun	Ernie	Bert	guitar	pigeon

 sings along too, until...**BOINGGG!**

 hears a kid on a . **BOING!** He hears the .

STRUM! He hears the  **COO!** And he hears his friend

, sounding sad.

"Oh dear," says . "I, , would like to make a noise

too. But sadly, my  will not hoot anymore."

Elmo hears another noise. **HONKKK!** That gives him an idea!

picture key

Elmo	pogo stick	guitar	pigeon	Grover	horn

 follows the noise down the street, until...**CLANGGG!**

 **CLANGS** the  of his trash can. And he **HONKS** a different kind of  .

" , would you share your  with  so he can make some noise too?"  asks.

"Well, all right," says  , handing the  to  . "The more noise the better!"

 **HONKS** his  .  **CLANKS** his  .

 **CLAPS** his  to join in!

" is glad he lives on such a noisy street,"  says. "Otherwise  might have stayed asleep and missed a great morning!"

picture key

Elmo	Oscar	lid	horn	Grover	hands

Breakfast Time

Mama Bear said to Goldilocks,

"What a nice surprise!

Pull up a chair. Here's a bowl.

Are they your just-right size?"

Elmo's mom said to Elmo,

"Well, you're up with the sun!

I like your smile at breakfast.

Good morning, little one!"

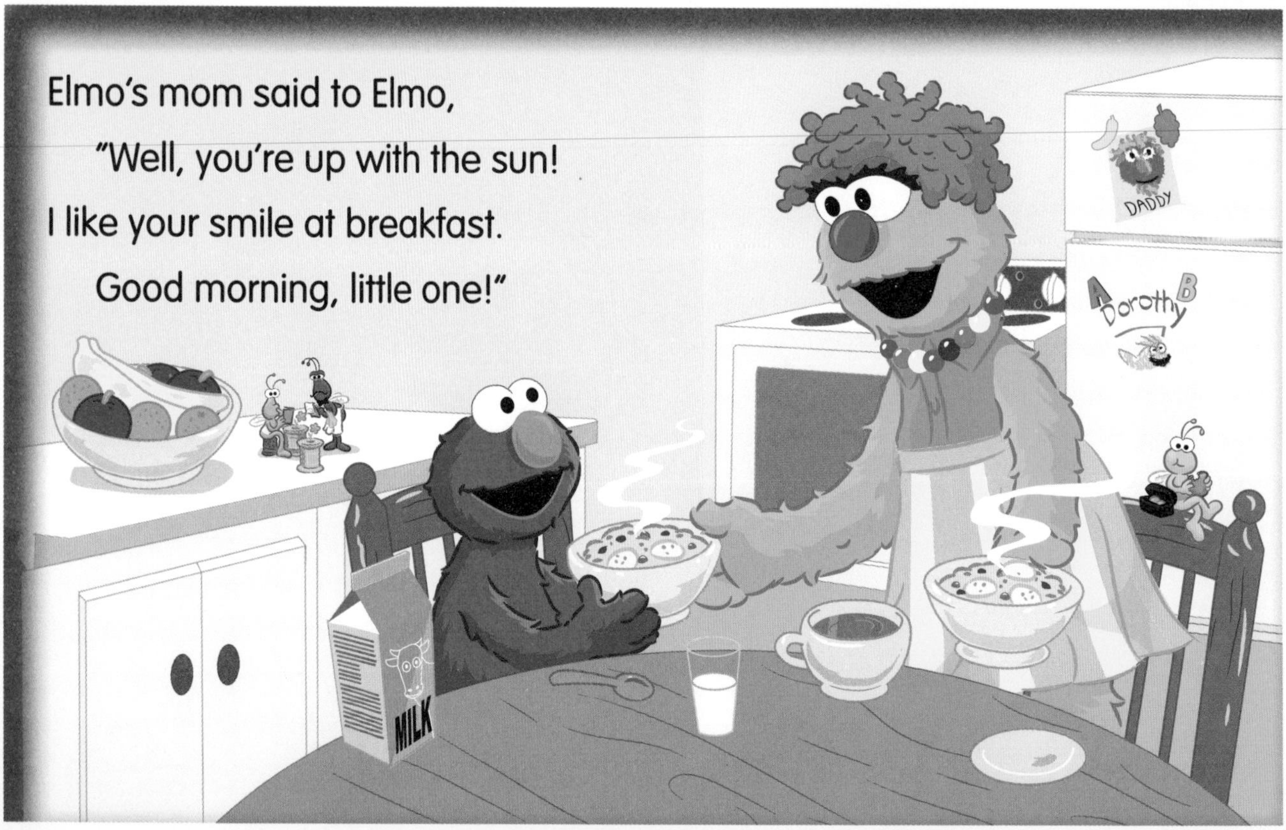

Goldilocks said to Mama Bear,
"My bowl is squeaky clean!
I really like your porridge,
hot or cold or in-between."

Elmo said to Elmo's mom,
"This porridge is so yummy!
May Elmo have a little more
to fill his hungry tummy?"

Whether you live on Sesame Street
or a place far, far away,
A healthy, hearty breakfast
is the way to start the day!

Elmo's Mixed-Up Day

Point to the pictures in the right order.

In the morning, Elmo:

goes to school

wakes up

plays with his friends

In the afternoon, Elmo:

slides down

sits on the slide

climbs the ladder

At night, Elmo:

brushes his teeth

gets into bed

puts on his jammies

Clean Dogs

brought to you by the letters **C** and **D**. Tap each one you find!

CLOUD

CAR

DIG

COW

DIRT

CAT

DOG

DUCK

Barkley digs daily, determined to discover treasure. How can his comrades get him clean?

Look and Find

Goodbye, Mommy! Goodbye, Daddy! Now it's time to go to school. Find these things Elmo will see in and around his classroom:

Under the Bed

Hello, everybodeee! It is I, Grover, all ready for bed. I have on my adorable pajamas. I have brushed my little teeth and washed my furry little face. Now I must get my fuzzy-wuzzy teddy bear. Then I will be all ready for bed.

Hmmm. There may be one teeny-tiny little problem. I looked under the covers, but my snuggly-wuggly teddy bear is not there. I looked in all of my drawers and all of my cabinets, but he is not there either.

Your furry friend, Grover, is running out of ideas. Can you think of any other place to look? Where, oh where can my teddy bear be? What did you say?

UNDER the BED?

Oh my goodness. I could not possibly look there! It is so very dark under the bed, especially at nighttime. Absolutely not.

What if there is something scary under the bed like—gulp!—a large, scary spider? And what if...what if the large, scary spider says something scary, like "Boo!"? Oh! I am frightened just thinking about it! Are you?

What did you say?

What if my itty-bitty teddy bear is frightened **TOO**?

I **MUST** look under the bed! I must rescue my frightened little teddy bear friend!

But first, I must be prepared. I will need a helmet in case the large, scary spider tries to tap dance on my head. I will need goggles in case the large, scary spider tries to—gasp!—look at me. I will need a flashlight to see if the large, scary spider is trying to look at me. And, of course, to see my dear teddy bear.

Hang on, little teddy bear. I, Grover, am coming to get you!

Goodness, look at all these nice toys under here. Maybe I should visit them more often.

And, look! My fluffy-wuffy teddy bear. Thank goodness, he does not look frightened. He looks happy as always. And a little bit sleepy. I, Grover, am also sleepy. Should we stretch out under here?

What did you say?

Go to sleep on **TOP** of the bed?

Good idea! Nighty-night!

When bedtime comes,
some people count sheep.
But the Count counts bats
when *he* wants to sleep!

Count out loud with the
Count! Find **7** bats in the
Count's room.

Picture Story

My Pal

Someone on Sesame Street is having a surprise birthday party!

Usually hates surprises, and birthdays, and parties. But

this surprise birthday party is different. It's for his friend !

lifts the of his and looks around. He

wants to find the perfect to bring to the party.

"What's in this pile of ?" says . "Maybe there's

something grimy for . Hey, and grimy rhyme. I'll

write a birthday poem for my pal!"

picture key

Slimey	Oscar	lid	trash can	present	trash

 searches Sesame Street for more rhymes. At the pool,

he sees a kid with a toy , and  sitting in a .

 says, "  and  are rhymes."

At the park,  sees a big , and he sees his

reflection in a puddle. "  rhymes with ME," says .

Then  looks at his . It is time for the party!

picture key

Oscar	**boat**	**Bert**	**float**	**tree**	**watch**

"Surprise!" yells everyone. 🐛 smiles. He is really surprised!

After 🐛 blows out the candles on his 🍰, 😄 reads:

"I don't want a 🚤 or a 🐸.

A pretty 🌳 isn't for me.

Those things aren't gross or grimy.

But one thing I love...is my pal 🐛!"

picture key

🐛	🍰	😄	🚤	🐸	🌳
Slimey	**cake**	**Oscar**	**boat**	**float**	**tree**

Hey Diddle Diddle

Hey diddle diddle, the cat with the fiddle
sat down to play a tune.
The little dog laughed to see such fun,
and the cow jumped over the moon!
Hey diddle dunder, did you ever wonder
why the cow jumped over the moon?
She was on her way to see her friends,
the cat and the dish and the spoon!

Entertaining Flight

brought to you by the letters E and F. Tap each one you find!

ELM

FLY

EGG

EAR

FEATHER

FEED

EYE

FUR

Do not fear! An egg falling from an elm tree can't escape everybody's friend, Super Grover! He flies to the rescue. What an exceptional feat!

WHAT'S DIFFERENT?

When her friends score a point, Zoe cheers!
Spot 10 things that are different in the playground pictures.

Oscar loves slippery, slimy things like worms! That's why Oscar and Slimey are best friends! Oscar knows how to make pretend worms that look almost real.

Wiggly Worms

Here's how to do it:

The next time you have spaghetti for dinner, save a few pieces. Ask if you can borrow a big bowl from the kitchen. A grown-up can help you measure and mix.

Mix 1 cup of water and 1 cup of white vinegar in the bowl. Now, add 2 tablespoons of baking soda. Things will start to gurgle and fizz! Toss in the spaghetti and watch the "worms" wiggle. Pretty cool, right?

VINEGAR

BAKING SODA

What Is a Friend?

A friend will push your swing for you,
   or push a wheelchair along.
A friend will climb to reach your kite.
   A friend is someone who is **STRONG**.

A friend will teach you how to dance,
   or how to make a paper heart.
A friend will read some books with you.
   A friend is someone who is **SMART**.

A friend will save a seat for you,
and make sure you're not left behind.
A friend will bring you picnic treats.
A friend is someone who is **KIND**.

A friend is nice to all new kids,
and has fun trying something new.
A friend is **STRONG** and **SMART** and **KIND**.
A friend is someone just like **YOU**!

Elmo's Friends

Elmo has a new camera! He wants to take a picture of his friend Zoe to put up on his wall.

"Say cheese, Zoe!" says Elmo.

But just as Elmo snaps the picture, Oscar pops up in front of Zoe and says, "SCRAM!"

Oops. Elmo did not get a picture of Zoe. He feels a little sad.

When Elmo sees Zoe at the beach, he tries again.

"Say cheese, Zoe!" says Elmo.

But just as Elmo snaps the picture, Cookie leans over to get some cookies.

Uh-oh! Elmo did not get a picture of Zoe this time either.

At the playground, Elmo sees Zoe on the swings.

"Say cheese, Zoe!" says Elmo.

But just as Elmo snaps the picture, Big Bird gives Zoe's swing a big push. Oh no! Elmo STILL did not get a picture of Zoe!

Elmo has an idea. Instead of taking a picture of just one friend, he will take pictures of lots of friends. And he will take pictures of interesting things all around Sesame Street.

The tunnel slide is a cool shape. And just as Elmo snaps the picture, out pops...Zoe!

Elmo looks at all the pictures he took and gets a big surprise. They didn't turn out the way he planned—they turned out even better. Now he has pictures of lots of friends, including Zoe!

"I'm proud of you," his mommy says. "You didn't give up. Now say cheese, Elmo!"

Elmo is going to give THIS picture to Zoe!

Count with the Count

Friends can have fun
in the sea or on land,
When we're wet from the ocean
or covered in sand!

Count along with the Count
to find:

1 lobster

2 sea stars

3 dolphins

4 clouds

5 seagulls

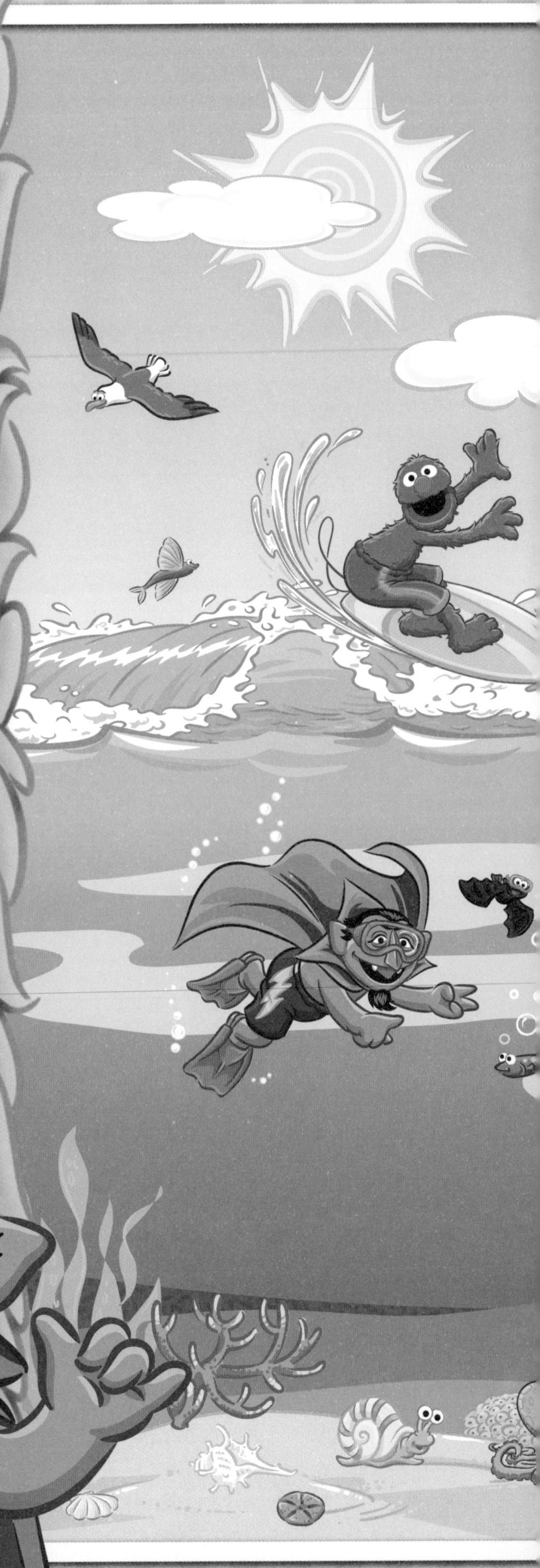

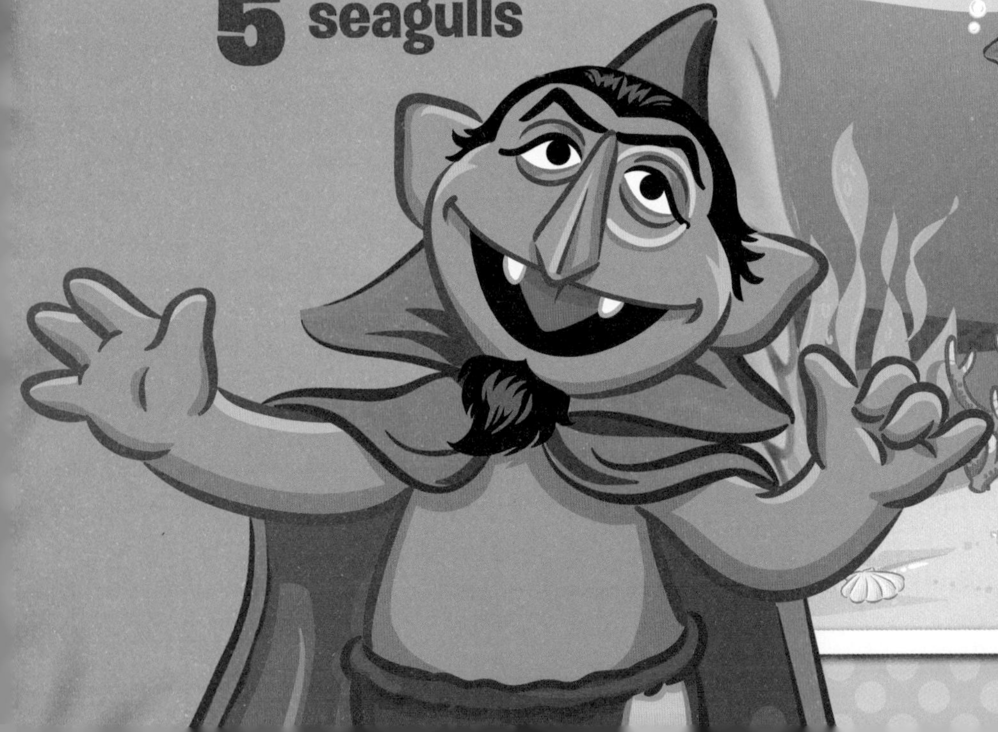

Picture Story

Go Away, ☁️!

🔴 lies in 🛏️, but it's hard to sleep. He is too excited

for tomorrow's trip to the water park. 🔴 can't wait to ride

down the giant water 🛝 and splash in the 🌊 pool.

"Tomorrow is going to be the best day ever!" says 🔴 as he

finally closes his 👀.

picture key

| rain | Elmo | bed | slide | wave | eyes |

Morning is here!  grabs his  and .

Then he hears thunder and .

"The water park is closed today," says .

"But  really wants to go to the water park and splash in the  pool,"  says sadly. "  doesn't want to stay inside and do nothing."

picture key

Elmo	swimsuit	snorkel	rain	Mommy	wave

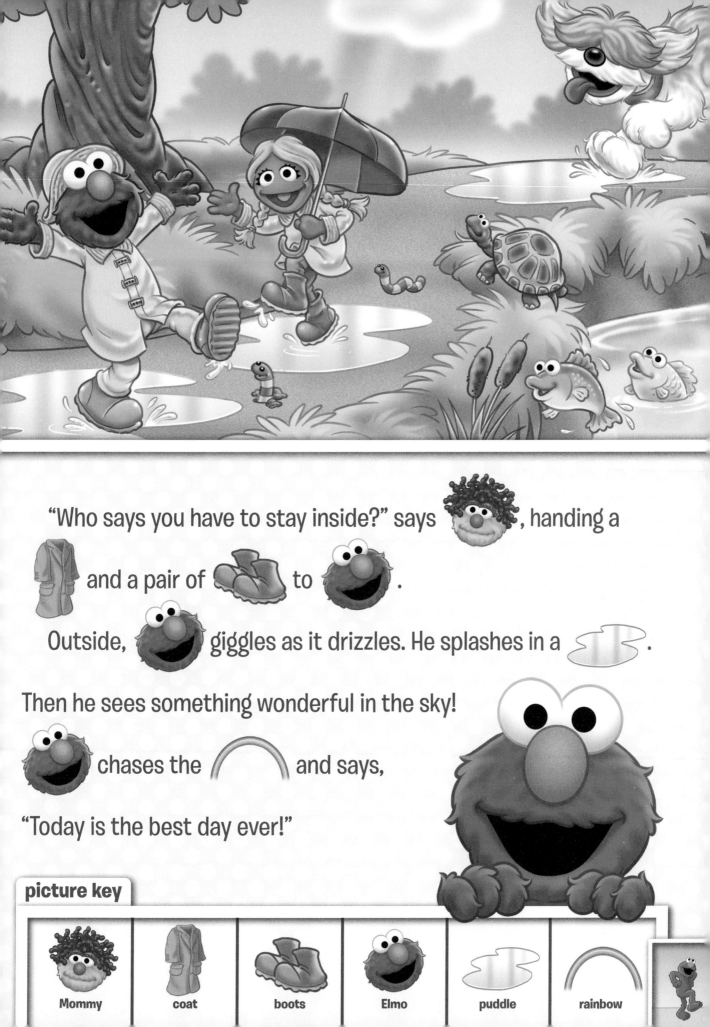

"Who says you have to stay inside?" says 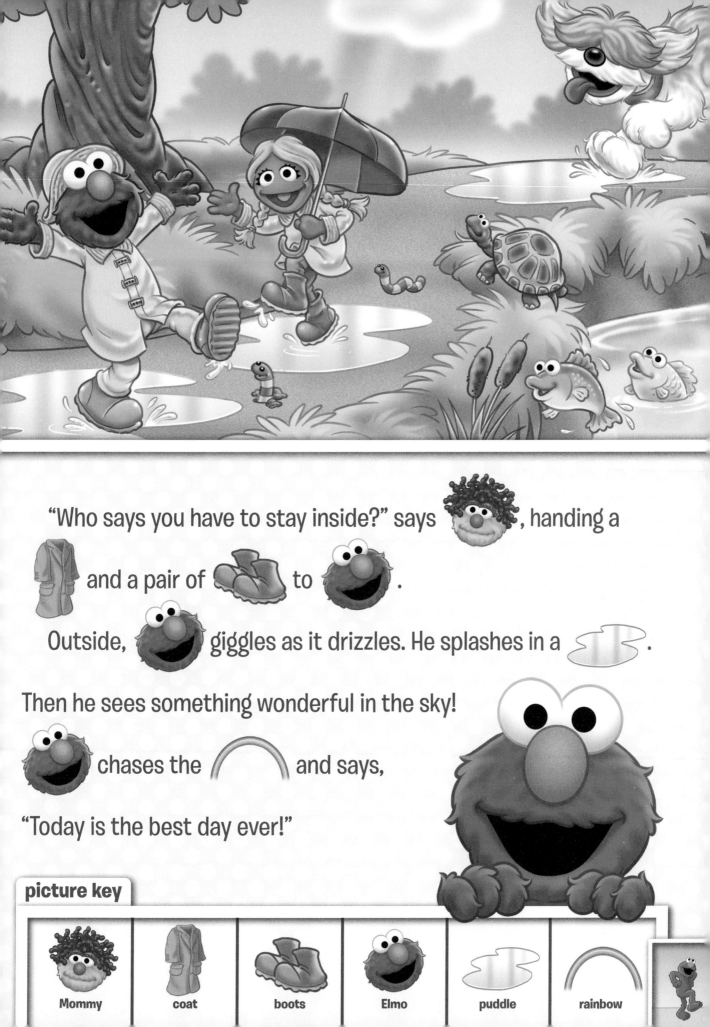, handing a and a pair of to .

Outside, giggles as it drizzles. He splashes in a .

Then he sees something wonderful in the sky!

 chases the and says,

"Today is the best day ever!"

picture key

Mommy	coat	boots	Elmo	puddle	rainbow	

Home Runs in Green Grass

brought to you by the letters G, H, and I. Tap each one you find!

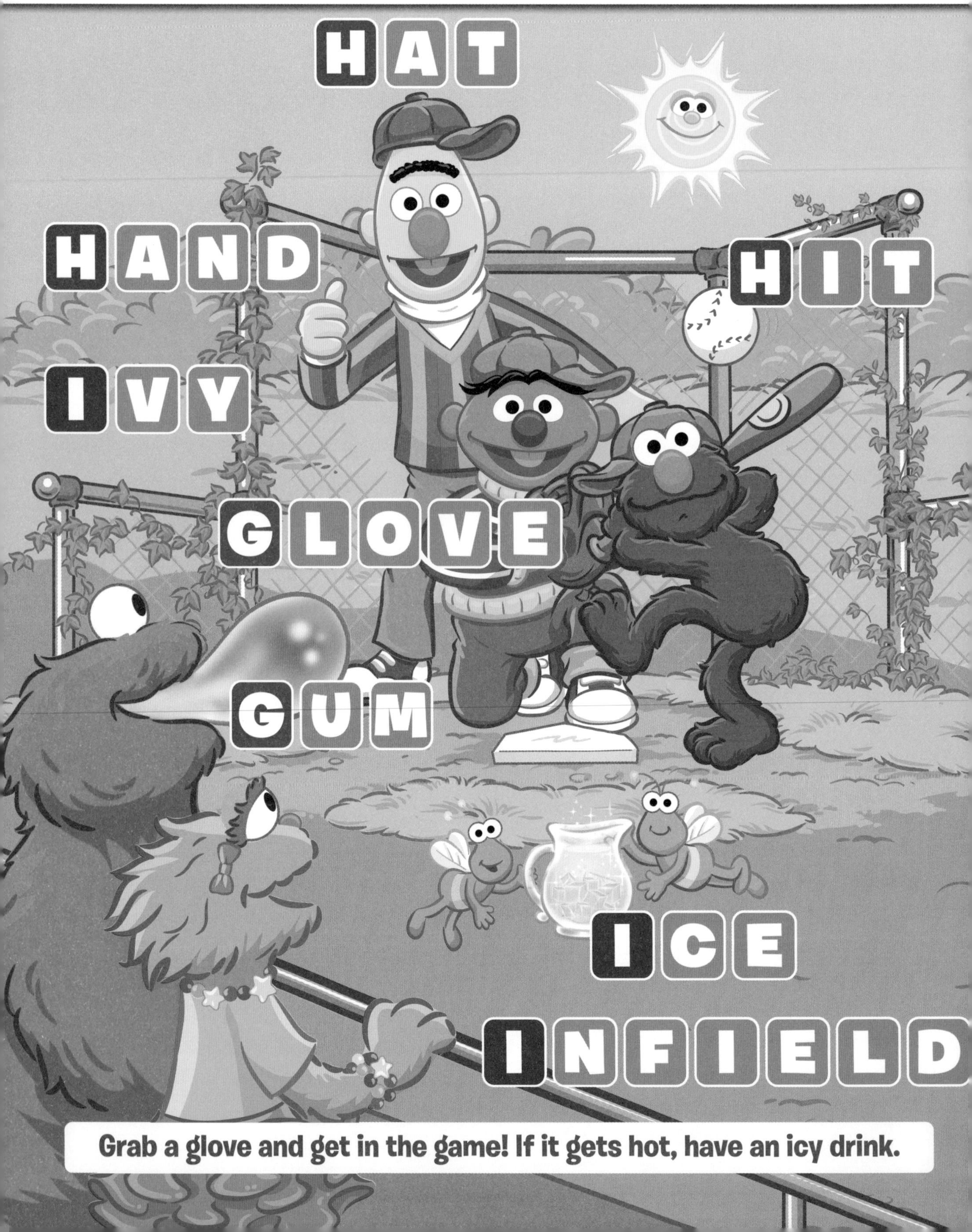
HAT
HAND
HIT
IVY
GLOVE
GUM
ICE
INFIELD

Grab a glove and get in the game! If it gets hot, have an icy drink.

Ernie, I don't believe you can make pepper move without pushing it!

Presto-shazamo!
I'll show you!

Pepper Magic

Here's how to do it:

Fill a bowl with water. *Shhh!* Here's the secret. Rub a little dishwashing soap on your finger. Sprinkle black pepper into the middle of the water. Dip your finger into the center of the peppery water. Watch the pepper move away from your finger!

SOAP

This looks like magic, but it's science at work! Water likes to stick to itself. (Scientists call that **cohesion**.) The top surface of water is *so* sticky that it forms a kind of skin called **surface tension**. But if you add a little soap to water, it stops sticking together. The water droplets move apart, and the pepper moves with it!

Run, Ride, Swim, Hop

Elmo **RUNS** like a pup,
with four feet on the ground.
Faster and faster,
he runs round and round.

Elmo **RIDES** like the wind
as he pedals his feet.
Faster and faster,
he rides down the street.

Elmo **SWIMS** like a fish,
with his feet flapping free.
Faster and faster,
he swims in the sea.

Elmo **HOPS** like a frog,
one foot up in the air.
Faster and faster,
he hops here and there.

He **RUNS**, and he **RIDES**,
and he **SWIMS**, and he **HOPS**.
Elmo loves to move, but sometimes...
he **STOPS!**

What's harder to catch the faster you run?
A cold?
Some ZZZs?
Wrong!
What's harder to catch the faster you run? Your breath!
Sigh.
Exactly!

Ya gotta love this stuff—the batter is green! Heh heh heh!

Hop to it! Let's get moving and mix up a batch of...

Oscar's Leapin' Lily Pads

Little Spinach Pancakes

Ingredients:

2 cups baby spinach

¼ teaspoon sugar

2 eggs

⅛ teaspoon ground nutmeg

1 tablespoon melted butter

½ cup all-purpose flour

½ teaspoon salt

½ cup low-fat milk

8 slices of cheddar cheese

Directions:

1. Chop the spinach in a food processor. Add the eggs, butter, salt, sugar, and nutmeg to the processor and mix everything together. Add the flour and mix. Add the milk and mix again until the batter is smooth. Yum! Slimy!

2. Lay the cheese slices on a cutting board. Cut each slice into four small circles or other shapes. (You can save the scraps for another snack.)

3. Heat a non-stick skillet and brush it lightly with melted butter. Drizzle the batter into the skillet in circles about two inches across.

4. Cook for a minute or until the edges turn dull. Flip each lily pad, and top them with the cheese shapes. Cover and cook for half a minute or until the cheese melts. Mmmmelty cheese!

5. Move the lily pads to a plate and repeat the steps with the remaining batter. Makes 30 leapin' lily pads. Eat up!

Try, Try Again

"**H**i, Elmo!" says Prairie Dawn. "Do you want to jump rope with us?"

Elmo has never jumped rope before, but he would like to try. He holds the handles and starts to hop. HOP!...HOP!...Then he stops. Elmo is all tangled up. He tries again, and this time he jumps a little bit longer before he gets tangled up.

"Would you like to join our basketball game?" Big Bird asks Elmo.

Elmo has never played basketball before, but he would like to try. He takes the ball and starts to bounce it. DOWN!...UP!...Whump. The basketball rolls away. Elmo tries again, and this time he bounces the ball a little bit longer before it rolls away.

"Come and fly kites with me!" Zoe says to Elmo. Elmo has never flown a kite before, but he would like to try. He takes the string in his hand and runs as the kite catches the wind. FLY!...FLY!...Oh my. The kite is stuck in a tree. After Super Grover gets the kite down, Elmo tries again. This time, he flies the kite a little bit longer before it gets stuck.

"Elmo is not as good as everyone else at jumping rope, playing basketball, or flying a kite," Elmo says.

"Don't worry, you'll get better with practice," Zoe tells Elmo. "It took me a long time to learn how to fly a kite, and how to dance, and how to do lots of fun things. But I know one thing you're already really good at."

"What's that?" asks Elmo.

"Trying!" says Zoe.

Let's get up and go!
It's sunny outside.
Get your wheels rolling
and go for a ride!

Count along with the Count
to find these moving things:

1  **Super Grover**

2  **spiders**

3  **pigeons**

4  **butterflies**

5 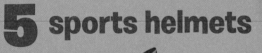 **sports helmets**

WHAT'S DIFFERENT?

After a day on the move, busy bodies need to rest! As Elmo snuggles in, see if you can spot 10 things that are different.

Sharing and Caring

Picture Story

Too Many 🍪 !

One morning, 🍪 places his trusty chef's 👨‍🍳 on his head

and makes his way to the kitchen. He grabs a big 🥣 , his lucky

🥄 , some flour, and some 🥚 .

"Me bake 🍪 !" says 🍪 .

But when it comes to 🍪 , sometimes 🍪 gets too

excited. "Maybe me make too many 🍪 ," says 🍪 . "Way,

way too many. Even for hungry monster!"

picture key

🍪	🍪	👨‍🍳	🥣	🥄	🥚	
cookies	Cookie Monster	hat	bowl	spoon	eggs	

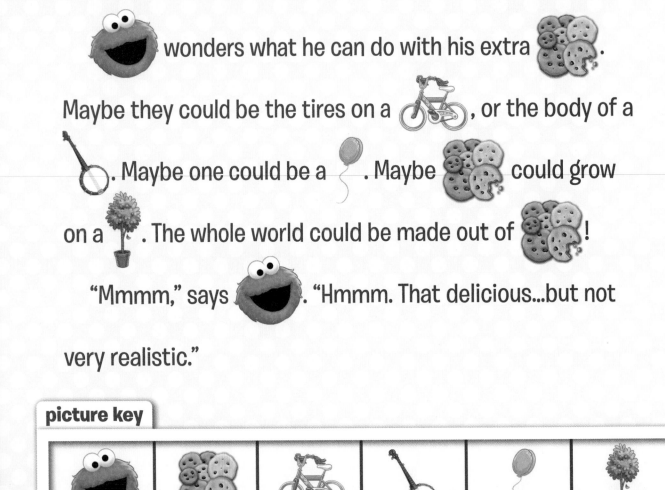

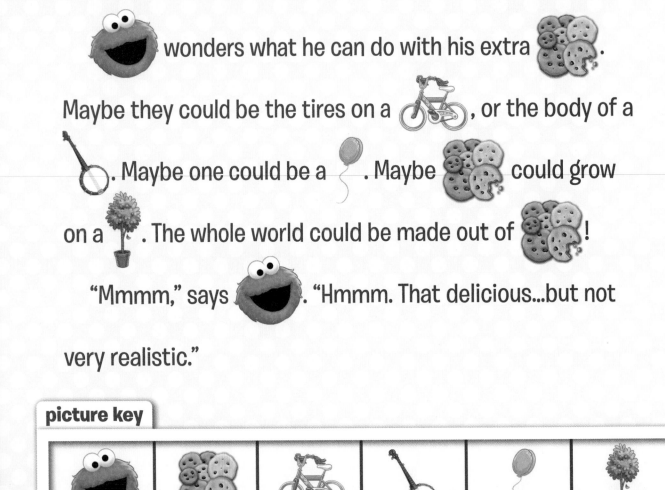 wonders what he can do with his extra .

Maybe they could be the tires on a , or the body of a

. Maybe one could be a . Maybe could grow

on a . The whole world could be made out of !

"Mmmm," says . "Hmmm. That delicious...but not

very realistic."

picture key

Cookie Monster	cookies	bicycle	banjo	balloon	tree

 has another idea. Instead of eating all the ,

or building a whole  out of , maybe he can *share*

his yummy  with his friends. , , and

 think that is a great idea.

"The only thing me love more than ," says ,

"is sharing ! Num, num, num."

picture key

Cookie Monster	cookies	world	Elmo	Grover	Zoe

Little Miss Muffet

Little Miss Muffet

   decided to rough it

by eating outside one day.

Along came a spider,

   who spoke when he spied her:

"Won't you please share your curds and your whey?"

Joyful Kids Laughing

brought to you by the letters **J**, **K**, and **L**. Tap each one you find!

KITE

LEAVES

LEG

JUMP

KID

JAR

LID

Bert gets a kick out of flying his kite. Next, he will kindly let Grover take a turn. While Grover waits, he laughs a lot, jokes, and jumps for joy!

Elmo loves his mommy, his daddy, baby David, and all his friends.

When you love someone, you want to share things with them. Like these yummy cookies!

Elmo's Hearty Oatmeal Hearts

Ingredients:

2 cups rolled oats
1½ cups all-purpose flour
½ cup whole-wheat flour
2 eggs
¾ cup white sugar

¾ cup brown sugar
1 cup butter, room temperature
2 teaspoons ground cinnamon
1 teaspoon baking powder

½ teaspoon cream of tartar
1 teaspoon vanilla extract
1 cup whole fresh or frozen cranberries

Directions:

1. Turn on the oven and set it to 350°F to heat up.

2. In a mixing bowl, stir the butter, white sugar, and brown sugar together. Then add the eggs and mix them in.

3. Add the cinnamon, baking powder, cream of tartar, and vanilla extract to the mixture. Next, stir in the oats, mix in both types of flour, and then add the cranberries.

4. Scoop up balls of dough about the size of a walnut. Put them in rows on a cookie sheet. Then put a heart-shaped cookie cutter around them and press the dough into the shape. If you don't have a heart-shaped cookie cutter, just use your hand to squish the balls down a little. Bake for 8 to 10 minutes.

5. Once the cookies have cooled, share them with your family and friends!

Playground games are a great time to share! Take a look at the photos and see if you can spot these things that monsters are sharing:

Let's Share

Oscar has **4** musical instruments. He plays **1** of them, so he has **3** to share. How many friends can he invite to play with him? Point to the picture of **3** friends.

Big Bird has **6** books. He wants to share them with Elmo, so they each get the same number of books. Point to the picture that shows **2** stacks of books that are the same. Count them!

Cookie Monster has a pizza. He wants to share it with his friends. He needs to cut it into **6** pieces. Which pizza has **6** pieces? Point to the picture.

Riddle-Rama

Toys for Twiddlebugs

Elmo and Abby have some new toys. They made the toys out of old things that nobody needs anymore. Elmo made a toy car out of a juice box. Abby made a playhouse out of a big cardboard box.

As they play, a Twiddlebug flies into Elmo's window. That gives Elmo an idea.

"Elmo and Abby have lots of toys now," says Elmo. "Let's collect old things that our friends don't need anymore and give them to the Twiddlebugs to make new toys!"

"Do you have anything you don't need?" Abby asks the Count.

"I have six bouncy balls," says the Count. "I have four pet bats. If I give one ball to each bat, I need four balls. You can have the two balls left over."

Cookie Monster has some celery stalks. He washes them and takes off the rubber band.

"Me eat celery," says Cookie, "but me *don't* eat rubber band. Here!"

Bert used to collect dominoes, but collecting bottle caps is more fun now. He gives Elmo and Abby some of his dominoes.

"Thanks, Bert," says Abby.

"Wait a minute," says Bert. "You can have some bottle caps too."

Oscar gives Elmo and Abby an ice pop stick and an empty spool. "Now scram," he says.

"Everyone on Sesame Street shared," says Elmo. "Now the Twiddlebugs can have toys and playhouses, too!"

Count with the Count

As the bus rolls along
down Sesame Street,
Each rider is ready
to share a seat!

Count out loud with the
Count! Can you find these
Sesame Street sights?

1 **Snuffleupagus**

2 **ice cream eaters**

3 **bus riders**

4 **birds**

5 **balloons**

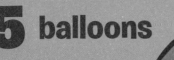

SUNNY DAY

123

A New

 is going to the park with her . "When will I be big enough to ride a ?"  asks.

"Today!"  tells her. "Surprise!"

 gives  a brand-new purple  with a big pink  and pink , and a pink .

 is so excited! But she is also a little bit scared.

"I'll be right beside you until you are ready to ride on your own,"  says.

At the park,  puts on her  nice and snug.

She climbs onto her . Then she says, "Ready, set, go!"

picture key

| tricycle | Zoe | Daddy | wheel | handlebars | helmet |

At first, [Daddy] holds onto the back of the [tricycle] while [Zoe] pedals slowly. Then [Zoe] pedals faster and faster, and before long she tells [Daddy] that he can let go.

"Wheee!" shouts [Zoe]. "I'm flying like a [bird]!"

As [Zoe] zooms along the path, she sees a friend. It's [Prairie Dawn].

She is riding a [bicycle], all by herself!

"[Daddy], when will I be big enough to ride a [bicycle]?" [Zoe] asks.

"Soon enough," [Daddy] says. "And when you are, I'll be right beside you until you are ready to ride on your own."

picture key

Daddy	**tricycle**	**Zoe**	**bird**	**Prairie Dawn**	**bicycle**

 rides her  around the park for a long time. Then  says, "It's time to go home."

They stop at the crosswalk and wait for the walk signal as a speedy green  zooms past.

"When will I be big enough to drive a ?"  asks.

"Soon enough,"  says. "Now let's cross the street. Walk right beside me." He pushes the  with one  and holds little  safely with the other.

"I'm big enough to ride a , and I'll be big enough to ride a  and drive a  someday,"  tells .

"But I will never be too big to hold your ."

picture key

Zoe	tricycle	Daddy	car	hand	bicycle

Little Red Riding Hood

Little Red Riding Hood loves visiting her grandmother. Grandma's home is warm and cozy. There is always something yummy just out of the oven. The walls are full of pictures of relatives from long ago, and Grandma tells the best stories about them. Most of all, Little Red loves having Grandma's attention all to herself…hey, wait a minute! Grandma has company! No fair!

"Hi, I'm Abby Cadabby," says Abby. "This Big Bad Wolf was going to trick you by pretending to be your grandma. And then he was going to eat you. So I turned him into a pumpkin."

"Oh, thank you!" says Little Red Riding Hood, and she gives Abby a hug.

"Ahem," says the wolf. "I'm not so big. And I'm not so bad. And I don't want to eat you. I really just wanted to try that pie your grandma baked. You see, I don't have a grandma…or anyone. I'm kind of a lone wolf."

"You poor thing!" says Little Red Riding Hood. "I'll share the pie. And the cookies. And my grandma, too. You can be a part of our family."

"You know, you remind me of a pet my great-great-uncle Bert had," Grandma says. "A gray goose…or was it a pigeon? Let's have some pie while I tell you all about him."

Monster Naptime

brought to you by the letters **M** and **N**. Tap each one you find!

MOO

MOON

NET

MOMMY

NECKLACE

NAP

Little monsters need naps nearly every afternoon.
Mommy's nice stories make naptime more magical.

WHAT'S DIFFERENT?

Families care, families share, and families have fun together! The Twiddlebug family is right at home in Ernie's window box. Can you find 5 differences between the pictures?

Together at Heart

Sometimes you have to say goodbye
to someone you hold dear,
But there are lots of ways to make
a faraway someone feel near.

You can make a special drawing
to give both of you a smile.
You can talk or text or chat on screen,
for a little while.

You can eat a special treat
   you both find tasty and nutritious.
A meal you've had together
   is a memory that's delicious!

You can look up at the moon,
   and as the moon shines down on you,
Remember that the same moon shines
   upon your loved one, too!

Look and Find

When Hannah got a new baby brother, Hannah's dad got a new camera! Can you find all these things in the baby pictures?

Welcome, BABY!

Mommy Loves Elmo

Do you know how much I love you, Elmo?

Would you love Elmo if he was...

...ten feet tall?

...or really, really small?

Bright stars are twinkling
high overhead.
Elmo is sleepy.
He is ready for bed.

His mommy and daddy
have tucked him in tight,
and wished him a cozy, warm,
dreamy good night.

Count along with the Count
to find these nighty-nighttime
things:

1 alarm clock

2 bunny slippers

3 blocks

4 storybooks

5 stars

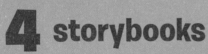

Picture Story

 and

 opens up his  and starts to read. He laughs right out **LOUD**. The  is really funny.

"Shhh,"  whispers, pointing to a . "The  says '**QUIET** Please.' Other  in the library are trying to read."

"Sorry,"  says. "I promise not to laugh anymore."  picks up another . He makes a **LOUD** yelp, and jumps up in his  with a **LOUD** thump. This  is a little bit scary.

"Shhh," says , pointing to the  again.

picture key

Ernie	Bert	book	sign	monsters	chair

At home,  and  make dinner.  slices a , a , and some . Then he tosses the veggies into a big, shiny bowl.

"Oops," says , as the , , and  tumble to the floor.

"Now the kitchen is too **MESSY**," says . He grabs a  to wash the floor and make the kitchen nice and **NEAT**.

picture key

Bert	Ernie	cucumber	pepper	carrots	mop

After dinner,  organizes his PAPER CLIPS and bottle caps.

 plays a jazzy tune on his horn with Rubber Duckie.

 is **LOUD** and **MESSY**.  is **QUIET** and **NEAT**.

The thing  likes best is to sit and sort PAPER CLIPS.

likes to dance around with Rubber Duckie.

 and  are very different, but there is one thing

they always agree on: they are best friends!

picture key

| Bert | paper clips | bottle | Ernie | horn | Rubber Duckie |

Jack and Jill

Jack and Jill went **UP** the hill
to fetch a pail of water.
Jack fell **DOWN**. He's such a clown!
And Jill came tumbling after.

When Jack fell down, he didn't **FROWN**.
He started to **SMILE**, you see.
He said to Jill, "Come down the hill,
and **YOU** can laugh with **ME**!"

PLEASE STAND BY

We interrupt our regularly scheduled "Brought to You by the Letter..." to bring you this special installment of "Big Bird's Words!"

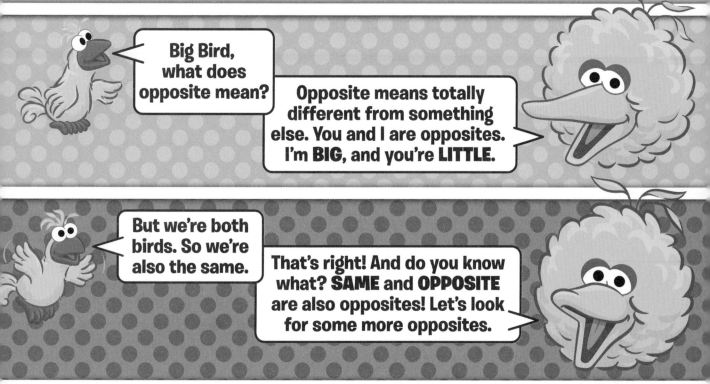

Big Bird, what does opposite mean?

Opposite means totally different from something else. You and I are opposites. I'm BIG, and you're LITTLE.

But we're both birds. So we're also the same.

That's right! And do you know what? SAME and OPPOSITE are also opposites! Let's look for some more opposites.

Point to each pair of opposites:

happy	hot	down
full	sweet	open
stop	day	big

night	sour	little
up	cold	go
empty	closed	sad

Elmo wants to take pictures of opposites! He looks **UP** and **DOWN** and all around. Can you help Elmo find things that are:

INSIDE Elmo's room

OUTSIDE Elmo's room

ABOVE the window

BELOW the window

in **FRONT** of Elmo

BEHIND Elmo

IN the bookcase

OUT of the bookcase

Me Hungry

Me find lots of opposites
    while me eat something yummy.
See? Me now have **EMPTY** plate
    and furry, **FULL** round tummy.

Me feel very **HAPPY** now,
    but others look **UPSET**.
Me try **REMEMBER** it their food...
    but sometimes me **FORGET**.

Me see another opposite:
me neat and **CLEAN** friend Grover.
His customer all **MESSY** now
when Grover spill food over.

Me ate up great **BIG** dinner.
It closing time already!
But maybe me have time for just
a **LITTLE** more spaghetti?

BIG and Little

Elmo hears Big Bird and Abby playing outside. He wants to play too! But first, he is going to take a picture of his friends. He rushes outside with his camera.

"Say cheese!" says Elmo. "Um, Big Bird needs to bend down a little." Big Bird bends down a little.

"Um, Big Bird needs to bend down a lot," says Elmo.

Big Bird bends down a lot. But no matter how hard Elmo tries, he can't fit both Abby and Big Bird into the picture.

"That's OK," Elmo says. "Let's go to the park to play hide-and-seek. Elmo will be 'It.'"

Elmo closes his eyes and counts to 10. Abby ducks behind a slide. But Big Bird can't find anything BIG enough to hide behind.

"I'm too BIG to do anything," Big Bird says sadly. "I wish I was little like you two."

"But you can do lots of things that little guys can't do," says Abby.

"BIG guys are good at shooting baskets," says Elmo. "When Elmo and his friends play basketball after school, everyone wants to be on Big Bird's team."

"We Birds are good at basketball," Big Bird says. "My cousin Larry played professionally."

"And we all love your extra-BIG pushes on the swings!" says Abby.

"Elmo remembers when Big Bird taught him how to roller skate," says Elmo. "Big Bird has a really BIG heart."

"I guess it's not so bad to be BIG," Big Bird says, "because I can give my little friends a great BIG hug!"

Elmo Knows How

Elmo knows how to draw **STRAIGHT** and **WIGGLY**.

Abby knows how to paint **LIGHT** and **DARK**.

Abby knows how to swing **HIGH** and **LOW**.

Grover knows how to climb **ON** and **OFF**.

Zoe knows how to dance **FAST** and **SLOW**.

Elmo knows how to play **LOUD** and **SOFT**. Now you try it!

Compared to Big Bird,
   Elmo is small.
But compared to a Twiddlebug,
   Elmo is tall!

Count and compare along
with the Count.

Count **3** knights.
Are there more purple knights
or red knights?

Count **5** blocks.
Are there fewer alphabet blocks
or number blocks?

Count **7** crayons.
Are there more blue crayons
or purple crayons?

Count **9** Twiddlebugs.
Are there fewer green Twiddlebugs
or yellow Twiddlebugs?

 for Everyone

"**M**e love !" says . "Good thing me  chef." He puts on his chef . Chef  has a big order.  is having a party with **10** guests, and they each want one of his famous  pies!

"Me need to make **10**  pies,"  says. "It easy to remember **10**. Me have **10** ."

picture key

				**10**	
pizza	Cookie Monster	hat	Grover	ten	fingers

First, Chef 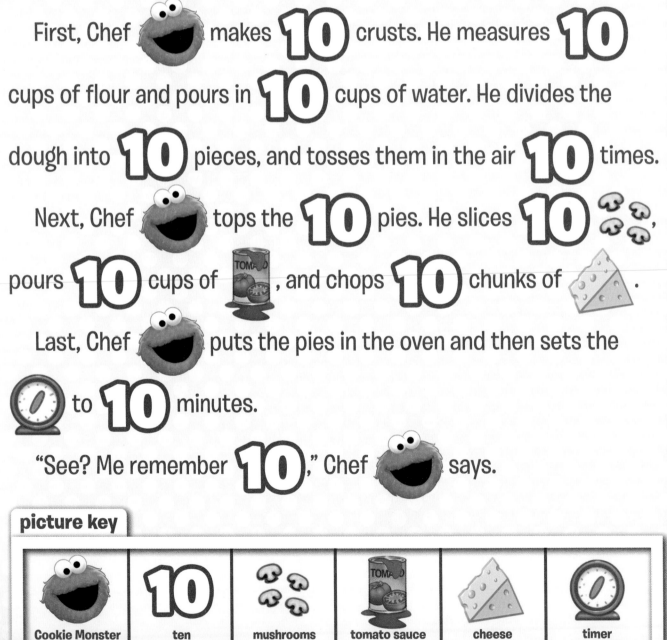 makes **10** crusts. He measures **10** cups of flour and pours in **10** cups of water. He divides the dough into **10** pieces, and tosses them in the air **10** times.

Next, Chef makes tops the **10** pies. He slices **10** , pours **10** cups of , and chops **10** chunks of .

Last, Chef puts the pies in the oven and then sets the to **10** minutes.

"See? Me remember **10**," Chef says.

picture key

Cookie Monster	ten	mushrooms	tomato sauce	cheese	timer

Chef  carries each  outside and counts, "One, two, three, four, five, six, seven, eight, nine, **10**... huh? No  for me? Me need one more  so me don't forget to count ME!"

"You can have a slice of my ," says .

"And mine," says .

Everyone shares a slice of  with . He ends up with **10** slices!

"That lot of ," says . "Even for me."

picture key

Cookie Monster	pizza	ten	finger	Abby	Grover

Hansel and Gretel

Hansel has a growling tummy.
Gretel thinks this house looks yummy.
They can't wait to eat a snack
from the witch's candy shack.

Cookie, cake, or lollipop?
They choose just one, and then they stop.
Everyone likes a "sometimes sweet,"
and witches don't mind if it's just one treat!

Outstandingly Perfect Quizzes

brought to you by the letters **O**, **P**, and **Q**. Tap each one you find!

P E A C H

P E A R

O R A N G E

Elmo

O W L

P I E

Q U A R T

perfect

Q U I Z

Elmo opens his backpack and pulls out a perfect quiz! He quickly places it on the fridge, and then picks a pear to eat.

From Farm to Table

Point to the pictures in the right order.

To grow food, we:

plant the seeds

harvest the crops

water the ground

To get milk, we:

collect the milk

milk the cow

take a drink

For dinner, we:

eat a meal

compost the scraps

shop for food

Big Bird's Words

Big Bird, what does **compost** mean?

Little Bird, **compost** means gathering the parts of food we don't eat, waiting for it to break down, and then adding it to the soil to grow more food.

And then what do we do with *that* food?

We eat it, and then **compost** the part we don't eat, so we can grow more food.

And then what do we do with *that* food?

We eat it, and then **compost** the part we don't eat, so we can grow more food.

And then what do we do...

Let's go have a snack, Little Bird.

Me famous for eating cookies. But even COOKIE Monster like a change sometimes, so long as it yummy...like crunchy, creamy dip!

Num, num, num!

Apple-tizing Apple Dip

Ingredients:
2 apples (different varieties)

1 cup yogurt

½ cup whole grain cereal or granola

dash of cinnamon

Directions:
1. Put the cereal between two paper towels.

2. Use a big spoon or your hands to mash and smash the cereal. Such fun!

3. Put the crushed-up cereal in a small bowl.

4. In another small bowl, stir the yogurt and a dash of cinnamon together.

5. Wash the apples and ask a grown-up to cut them into slices.

6. Sprinkle the cereal on top of the yogurt dip, scoop the dip onto an apple slice, and *num, num, num*!

Look and Find

When it's time for snacks at school,
healthy munchies are the rule.
Apples and carrots are tasty fuel.
Eating well is really cool!

Can you find all of these
tasty treats?

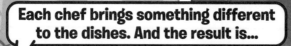

"*Ah ah ah!* Let's count some foods
that make a colorful sight
Before these hungry shoppers
    stop and take a great big bite!"

1 blue food

2 yellow foods

2 purple foods

2 red foods

2 orange foods

3 green foods

Shapes and Colors

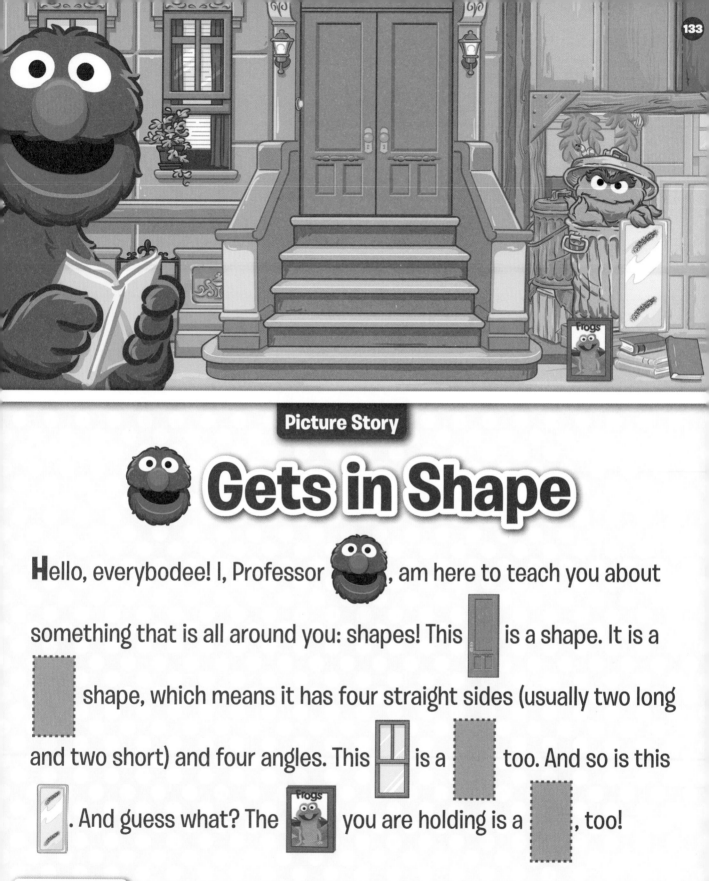

Picture Story

Gets in Shape

Hello, everybodee! I, Professor 🟦, am here to teach you about something that is all around you: shapes! This 🚪 is a shape. It is a ▭ shape, which means it has four straight sides (usually two long and two short) and four angles. This 🪟 is a ▭ too. And so is this 🪞. And guess what? The 📖 you are holding is a ▭, too!

picture key

Grover	door	rectangle	window	mirror	book

Even  likes shapes...well, shapes that are in and around his trash can, like this tossed-out slice of pizza. The pizza is shaped like a triangle, which means it has three sides and three angles.

This half of a sandwich is also a triangle shape. And this watermelon slice looks like a triangle, too. But not for long, because I am going to take a big bite out of it! Bye-bye, triangle.

picture key

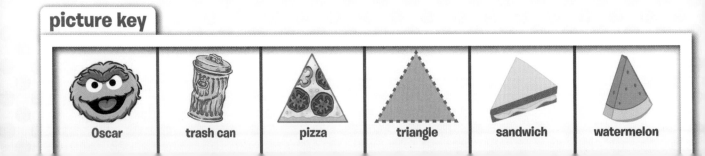

| Oscar | trash can | pizza | triangle | sandwich | watermelon |

Now it is time for some 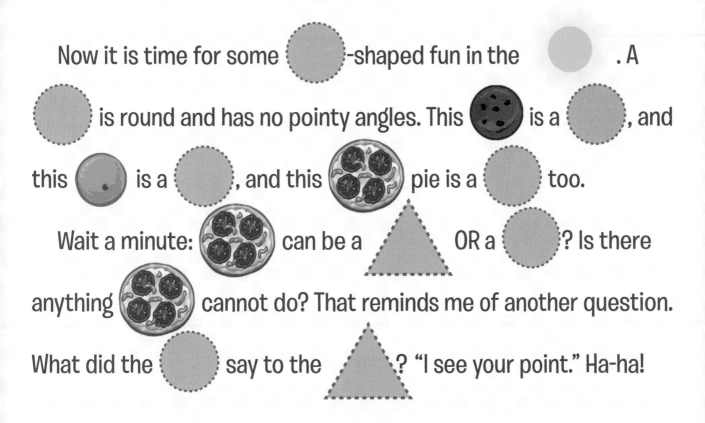-shaped fun in the ⬤ . A

⬤ is round and has no pointy angles. This 🍪 is a ⬤ , and

this 🟠 is a ⬤ , and this 🍕 pie is a ⬤ too.

Wait a minute: 🍕 can be a ▲ OR a ⬤ ? Is there

anything 🍕 cannot do? That reminds me of another question.

What did the ⬤ say to the ▲ ? "I see your point." Ha-ha!

picture key

circle	sun	cookie	orange	pizza	triangle

Prince Elmo and the Pea

It's time for Prince Elmo to climb into bed, with a soft feather pillow for his sleepy head.

But something is bumpy and poking his back under the mattresses in a tall stack.

Elmo tosses and turns. What could it be? Now it's poking his elbow, his tummy, his knee!

Is it a **square**, a **star**, or a **heart**?
Elmo knows shapes. He can tell
them apart!

This thing is smooth. Like a ball, it is round.
Elmo hops out of bed and onto the ground.

Under the mattress, now
what does he see?
Elmo sees a green **circle**.
Why, he sees…a pea!

Really Sunny Times

brought to you by the letters **R**, **S**, and **T**. Tap each one you find!

SUN

SKY

RAY

SEA

TUB

ROW

TWO

RED

ROUND

STAR

Telly relishes summer skies and rollicking rides in a trustworthy tub. He is strong as he rows along in the tide.

What is a *prism*? Rosita knows! Elmo knows too. A prism is something clear that breaks clear light into all the colors of the rainbow. Do you want to make a rainbow with Rosita?

Rainbow in a Jar

Here's how to do it:

Ask a grownup to help you fill a glass jar with water.
Put the jar on a windowsill in bright sunlight.
Put a sheet of white paper on the floor in front of the window.

Do you see a rainbow on the paper? What colors do you see? The name **ROY G. BIV** will help you remember them in order: **R**ed, **O**range, **Y**ellow, **G**reen, **B**lue, **I**ndigo, **V**iolet!

WHAT'S DIFFERENT?

I, Grover, think green is keen! Can you find 10 things that are different between one green scene and the other?

Elmo peeks out of
a window that's **square**.
What colors and shapes
does he see from up there?

A **yellow** **circle** sun
shines high in the sky.
A **red** **rhombus** kite
flies swiftly on by.

This **orange** shape is a ball.
Like a **circle**, it's round.
It hits the **rectangle** backboard,
and then falls to the ground.

On **red** **rectangle** slats,
Big Bird likes to hop!
A **red** **octagon** sign
tells the bikes when to stop.

STOP

Triangle-shape sides
form this sandy **gold** tower.
Cookie eats **circle** cookies.
It's the snack-time hour!

So Many Colors

Yay! It's time for art class. Abby Cadabby loves art, even though it doesn't use magic. Today the art teacher asks the class to paint pictures of their favorite animals.

"I have so many favorite animals," Abby thinks while Mr. Stevenson hands out supplies. "I want to paint them all!"

Abby looks at her paint palette and sees three paint colors: red, yellow, and blue. She paints a red crab, a yellow chick, and a blue parrot. Then she raises her hand.

"I'm all done!" Abby tells the teacher.

"You used all three colors on your paint palette," says Mr. Stevenson. "Good job! But did you know that you can mix those three colors to make even more colors?"

Abby did not know that! But she is excited to try it. First, she mixes red and yellow. That makes orange, like a tiger! Next, she mixes yellow and blue. That makes green, like a frog! Finally, she mixes red and blue. That makes purple, like the cute little sea horse in the classroom aquarium.

Abby paints an orange tiger, a green frog, and a purple sea horse. Then she raises her hand again. "I'm all done again!" she tells the teacher.

Mr. Stevenson looks at Abby's animal paintings. "You made three more colors for your paint palette," he says. "Nice work! Now, are you sure you have done every possible color mixture?"

"I think I did," says Abby. "Hey, wait a minute..." This time, Abby mixes red AND yellow AND blue. That makes brown, like a monkey! Abby paints a brown monkey. Then she raises her hand again. "Now I'm really all done!" she tells the teacher.

"Excellent!" says Mr. Stevenson. "Can you tell me what you learned today?"

"I learned that I can mix three colors to make four more colors," says Abby. "Wow, that's so magic!"

Count with the Count

"I love counting shapes,
  whether pointy or round,
Or up in the sky,
  or down on the ground!"

Can you find and count objects
with these shapes?

1 oval   **3** rhombuses

2 triangles   **4** circles

Picture Story

 Joins the Band

 is learning about music at school.  loves music.

He wants to be the lead singer in a rock 'n' roll band.  will

play the . Rat-a-tat!  will play the . Ring-a-ling!

 will sing on a great big stage.

"Some , a singer, and one measly ?" says .

"You call that a rock 'n' roll band? Scram!"

picture key

Oscar	Elmo	Cookie Monster	drums	Zoe	tambourine

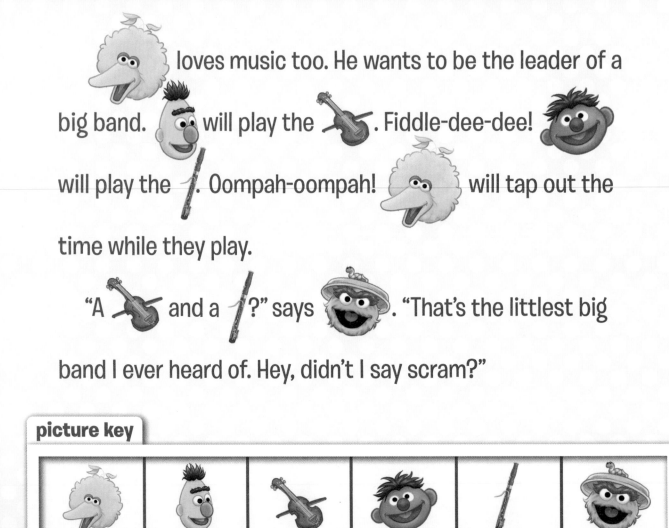

 loves music too. He wants to be the leader of a big band. will play the . Fiddle-dee-dee! will play the . Oompah-oompah! will tap out the time while they play.

"A and a ?" says . "That's the littlest big band I ever heard of. Hey, didn't I say scram?"

picture key

| Big Bird | Bert | violin | Ernie | bassoon | Oscar |

 and  start to scram, but as they do  steps on something shiny. It's a .

", is this your ?"  asks.

"As a matter of fact, it is,"  says.

"Do you want to be in one of our bands?"  asks.

"Well, I was kinda busy," says .

"But if you insist. I should mention that I play  and  too."

picture key

| Big Bird | Elmo | horn | Oscar | tambourine | maracas | |

Big Bird's Words

Did you know that **music** can change your **mood**? **Mood** is how you feel. Songs can be fast or slow, or loud or soft, or have a beat that makes you feel a certain way.

Unbelievable Virtuosos

brought to you by the letters **U** and **V**. Tap each one you find!

UKULELE

VIOLIN

UNIFORM

VOICE

This uptown venue is far from vacant when the Valiant Undertones venture to play their unique and vibrant verses.

For the Birds

Cheep! Chirp! Warble! Whistle! Elmo sings just like a bird!

Here's how to do it:

Collect some pinecones and corncobs, and get some long pieces of string. Tie a string to each pinecone and cob.

Use a spoon to spread vegetable shortening all over the pinecones and corncobs. Then roll them in birdseed.

Hang the pinecones and corncobs in places birds can reach, like trees or open porches.

Now sit outside and have a tuneful time! *Tweet-tweet!*

WILD BIRDS

BIRD SEED

Bird feeders are a great way to invite feathered friends to come visit and sing their pretty songs.

Do the Pigeon Peck Dance

So you think you don't know how to dance?
Come on, get up, and take a glance...

SPIN! SPIN!

SPIN! SPIN!

Do you see anything around YOU moving?
Move along! Soon you'll be grooving.

Elmo sees some pigeons on the street.
They peck and they flap. Elmo feels the beat.

They flap and they peck. So Elmo does too.
He flaps and he pecks while the pigeons coo.

"Flap, flap, peck!" Elmo chants and sings.
"Flap, flap, peck! Use your arms like wings."

"Peck, peck, flap! Just keep on trying.
Peck, peck, flap! Look, now you're flying!"

WHAT'S DIFFERENT?

Grover is grooving in the park! See if you can spot
10 things that are different in these dancing scenes.

Daytime Lullaby

One bright and sunny afternoon, Elmo visits the nature preserve. He likes to hear the chipmunks chatter and the chickadees chirp. But one part of the preserve is very, very quiet. Elmo looks around and notices an owl fast asleep in a tree.

"Is it the owl's naptime?" Elmo asks the friendly park ranger.

"It's the owl's bedtime," says the ranger. "Owls sleep all day and stay awake all night. They're nighttime animals."

Elmo has never heard of a nighttime animal. He thinks about it for a minute. "Nighttime animals must be very bored," he says, "because daytime is when all the fun things happen."

"Lots of things happen at night," says the park ranger. "Crickets croon and fireflies flicker. As the owl flies through the starry night sky, he might look down and see a family of opossums slinking about, or a raccoon out having a midnight snack."

"Wow, that sounds like FUN!" says Elmo. He says it so loudly that he wakes up the owl!

"Oh no!" says Elmo. "Elmo is sorry for waking you up, Mister Owl. Maybe a lullaby will help you fall back asleep."

"*Whoooo*," says the owl.

"Elmo will sing the lullaby!" says Elmo. He sings the sweetest, softest lullaby he knows. By the time he is finished singing, the owl is sleeping soundly...

And so is the park ranger!

The toe-tapping Twiddlebugs
are ready to spin.
And a-one, and a-two!
Bert counts them in.

Can you count these things
on the stage?

 trumpet

 Twiddlebugs

 spotlights

 cello strings

 music notes

In the Neighborhood

Picture Story

A Hike on ⟨SESAME STREET⟩

"**W**hat should we do today?" asks .

"Oh, why don't you all take a hike!" says 😈.

"Good idea!" says 🐱. "Let's take a *nature* hike!"

 wonders if they should hike in the forest or on a farm.

"We can take a nature hike right here on ⟨SESAME STREET⟩!" says 🐱.

"Aw, who needs nature when you can have 🗑 ?" 😈 growls.

"Go on, scram!"

picture key

⟨SESAME STREET⟩	Ernie	Oscar	Zoe	Grover	trash	
Sesame Street	Ernie	Oscar	Zoe	Grover	trash	

"How will we find nature on SESAME STREET?" asks Grover.

"Look at the leaves on these doors," Bert says. "The ivy is growing way up to the sky. And I see a bird! A city bird and Big Bird are right at home on SESAME STREET."

"SESAME STREET may not be a forest," says Grover, "but see that tree? And those bee-yootiful flowers?"

"The butterflies like the flowers too," says Ernie. "Hi, little guys."

picture key

SESAME STREET **Sesame Street**	**Grover**	**leaves**	**Bert**	**bird**
Big Bird	**tree**	**flowers**	**butterflies**	**Ernie**

"This city-grown  look mighty tasty," says .

"Num, num, num. Hey, what that on me ?"

"That's our pal !" says . "We're back where we started."

"I thought I told you to take a hike," says .

"We did!" says . "We followed nature up and down

SESAME STREET, right back here to YOU."

picture key

| tomato | Cookie Monster | Slimey | Zoe | Oscar | Sesame Street | |

Rosita and the Beanstalk

Once upon a time, there was a little monster named Rosita, who had a **BIG** problem. Her tummy was gr-r-r-r-rowling, and there was no food or money in her house.

The only thing Rosita had to sell was her cow. The farmer down the road wanted the cow. But he did not have any money either. Instead, he offered to trade some magic beans for the cow.

"How can beans be magic?" wondered Rosita. It wasn't long before she found out! In her garden, the beans grew into a **HUGE** beanstalk stretching way up high into the sky.

"How high does it go?" wondered Rosita, as she began to climb. The beanstalk led straight to a **GIGANTIC** castle.

"Who lives in such a place?" wondered Rosita. (In case you haven't noticed, Rosita was a very curious monster.) Inside the castle, she saw an **ENORMOUS** furry blue giant.

"Fee, fi, fo, num-num!" roared the giant. "Me think a little monster come. Where is monster?"

Uh-oh! Just at that moment, Rosita's tummy gave a **TREMENDOUS** *gr-r-r-r-rowl.*

"What will the giant do?" wondered Rosita. It wasn't long before she found out!

"Welcome, neighbor!" said the giant. "You just in time for lunch: **EXTRA-LARGE** scrambled golden eggs. And **COLOSSAL** cookies!"

Look and Find

Whenever Elmo takes a walk,
    he sees his neighbors on the block.
Some have two feet. Some have four.
    Some, like bugs, have even more!

Lots of monsters live on Sesame Street.
Lots of animals do, too! Can you
spot these animal friends in the
neighborhood?

Wonderful Examinations

brought to you by the letters **W** and **X**. Tap each one you find!

X-RAY

WINDOW

WALL

WHITE

WAG

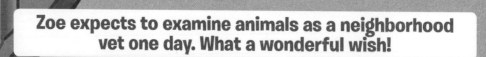

Zoe expects to examine animals as a neighborhood vet one day. What a wonderful wish!

Do you have a mountain in your neighborhood? Elmo doesn't! But there might have been a mountain in Elmo's backyard a long time ago. Where did it go?

Backyard Mountains

Here's how to do it:

In your yard or local park, build three mini-mountains: one out of rocks, one of sand, and one of dirt.

- Pour a cup of water over the sand mountain. How much of the mountain washed away?
- Pour a cup of water over the dirt mountain. How much washed away? Was it more or less than the sand?
- Pour a cup of water over the rock mountain. How much washed away? Did it erode at all? Was it more or less than the sand and dirt?

Water can make big things like boulders and mountains fall apart. It just takes a very long time. Try building some mini-mountains to see how this action, called **erosion**, works.

Elmo thinks it would take a very big, very long rainstorm to erode a mountain!

First Things First

On the Way Home

Elmo and his daddy had a fun morning at the fire station.
Now they want to get home in time for lunch!
They need to make three stops on the way.

START →

Use your finger.
Trace a route
through the
maze.

SESAME STREET POST OFFICE

HOOPER'S STORE

SUBWAY
1 2 A B

Which route is the quickest?

route 1

route 2

route 3

→ FINISH

Neighbors

On your sidewalks, on your street,
what do you hear? Who do you meet?

A bus driver takes you for a ride.
Honk-honk! Honk-honk! Just hop inside!

A construction worker might drill or dig.
Whirrrrrrr! Her tools are noisy and big.

A teacher helps you learn new things.
Ding-ding-ding! The school bell rings.

A doctor checks your ears and nose.
Lub-dub, lub-dub, your heartbeat goes.

A police officer guards, and protects.
Tweet-tweet! He stops cars. You cross next.

A firefighter keeps you safe from harm.
Clang-clang is the sound of the station alarm.

Say *hello* to the neighbors you meet
on your sidewalks, on your street.

Oscar's little corner
of Sesame Street
is filled with junk
he thinks is neat.

Count along with the
Count to find these things
in Oscar's trashy stash:

1 flowerpot
Is it bigger or smaller
than the trash cans?

2 banana peels
What color are they?

3 trash can lids
What sound would you hear
if you dropped one?

4 worms
Do they have stripes
or spots?

T'S THE PITS!

Out and About

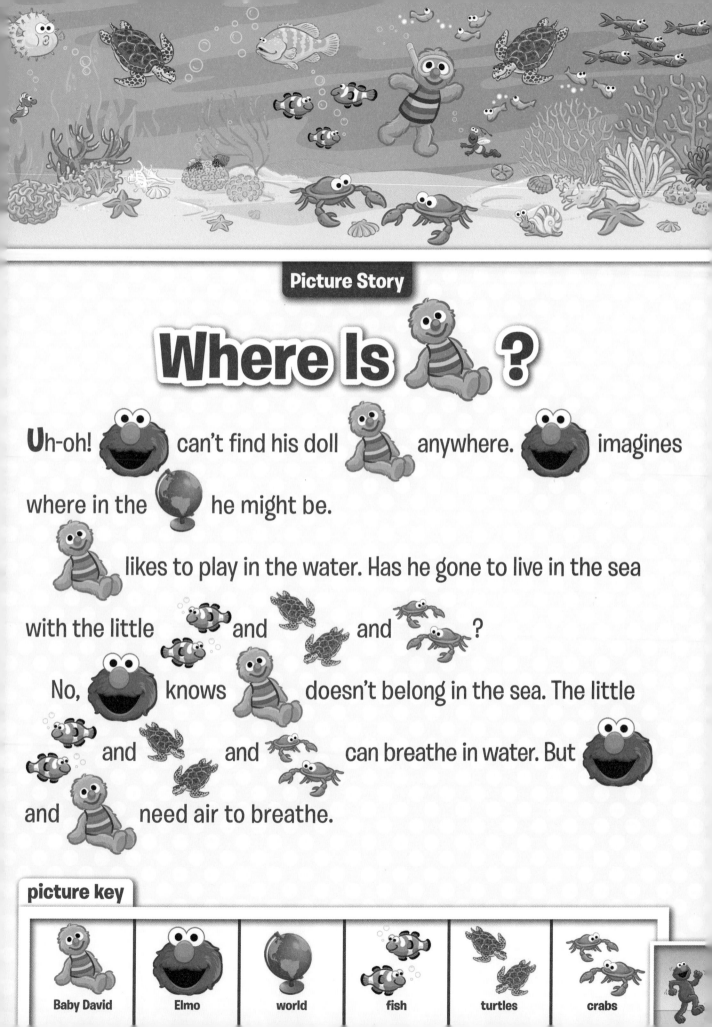

Where Is 🧸 ?

Uh-oh! 🔴 can't find his doll 🧸 anywhere. 🔴 imagines where in the 🌍 he might be.

🧸 likes to play in the water. Has he gone to live in the sea with the little 🐟 and 🐢 and 🦀 ?

No, 🔴 knows 🧸 doesn't belong in the sea. The little 🐟 and 🐢 and 🦀 can breathe in water. But 🔴 and 🧸 need air to breathe.

picture key

🧸	🔴	🌍	🐟	🐢	🦀
Baby David	Elmo	world	fish	turtles	crabs

 likes to play in the snow. Has he gone to live in Antarctica

with the little  ?

No,  knows  doesn't belong in Antarctica. The little

 are covered with special feathers that keep them warm.

Antarctica is too cold for  .

 likes to play in the trees. Has he gone to live in the jungle

with the little  and  and  ?

Maybe...but wouldn't  miss playing with  ?

picture key

| Baby David | penguins | Elmo | monkeys | tigers | elephants |

Suddenly  remembers something. He runs up the  to his room, looks under his  ...and finds  !

 and  were under the  pretending to explore a deep, dark cave when  called  down for dinner.

"Oh, , wherever you go in the whole ,"  says, " will go too. You and  belong together."

picture key

Elmo	stairs	bed	Baby David	Mommy	world

Twinkle, Twinkle Little Star

Twinkle, twinkle, little star,
Elmo wonders what you are!
Where are the facts he's looking for?
The Space Museum! Let's explore!

Big Bird's Words

Big Bird, what does it mean to explore?

Little Bird, when you explore, you set out to learn something you didn't know before.

Is Elmo going to explore the museum?

Yup. First, he'll explore displays about stars to see what they're made of. Then, he'll explore pizza in the café to taste what *it's* made of!

By the rings of Saturn, this pizza is out of this world!

Elmo's Space Pizza

Ingredients:

1 English muffin

1 can of tomato sauce

1 red, yellow, or green pepper

a handful of grape tomatoes

some shredded mozzarella cheese

a pinch of oregano

Directions:

1. One, two, three, blast off! Set the oven to 350°F and let it heat up.

2. Split the English muffin into two halves. Spread the rough side of each half with tomato sauce, and then sprinkle cheese and oregano on top of the sauce.

3. Ask a grown-up to cut the top and bottom off the pepper. You can help take out the seeds. The grown-up can slice the pepper into thin rings and cut the tomatoes in half the long way. Then you can put a few pepper rings and tomato halves on top of each muffin half.

4. Place the muffin halves on a cookie sheet (cheese side up!), and then slide the sheet into the oven.

5. Bake for 10 minutes, until the cheese is good and melty.

Young Zoo-goers

brought to you by the letters **Y** and **Z**. Tap each one you find!

ZOO

ZEBRA

YARD

YELLOW

YAK

ZIP

ZOE

Zoe zips around the zoo to see yaks, zebras, and yellow-feathered friends flying zigzag from here to yonder!

Goodbye! Hello!

Elmo is exploring Australia,
   Down Under.
He sees a strange something
   that makes him wonder.

What does it look like?
   A crooked stick.
Throw it far as you can.
   It flies back, quick!

It's a boomerang!
   Watch it go.
Then it's back again.
   Goodbye! Hello!

Captain Cookie wants to sail the ocean blue. He doesn't live near an ocean, but he can make a pretend ocean in a bottle. Oooh, cool!

Ocean in a Bottle

You'll need:
a clear plastic bottle with a cap
vegetable oil
blue food coloring
shells and glitter (if you like)
a funnel
water

Here's how to do it:
- Fill the bottle three-quarters full of water. Add blue food coloring and, if you like, shells and glitter too. That's your "ocean"!
- Place the funnel into the bottleneck and add the oil. That's your "sky"!
- Screw the cap on tightly and shake the bottle. Watch the oil and water mix for a second, then separate back into "ocean" and "sky."
- Turn the bottle on its side and rock it back and forth. You have ocean waves in a bottle!

Riddle-Rama

It is I, Super Grover, with a new riddle for you!

Go away! I'm busy writing a letter to complain about the garbage pickup around here. Can you believe it? The truck comes *every* week!

My timing is perfect! My riddle and your letter have something in common. What travels around the world, but always stays in one spot?

I don't know, but I'm sure you're gonna tell me.

A stamp!

How about mailing my letter for me as you scram your way past the post office?

A new year begins
when an old year ends.
In China, each year
has an animal friend.

From the Year of the Rat
to the Year of the Pig,
The New Year celebration
is always BIG!

Count out loud with the
Count to find these
12 animals at the parade:

rat	**dragon**	**monkey**
ox	**snake**	**rooster**
tiger	**horse**	**dog**
rabbit	**sheep**	**pig**